P9-EMP-287

DANCING TEEPEES

POEMS ✧ OF ✧ AMERICAN ✧ INDIAN ✧ YOUTH

DANCING TEEPEES

SELECTED BY

VIRGINIA DRIVING HAWK SNEVE

WITH ART BY

STEPHEN GAMMELL

HOLIDAY HOUSE ✧ NEW YORK

FRANKLIN PIERCE
COLLEGE LIBRARY
RINDGE. N. H. 0346

Curric
E
98
.P74
.D36
1989

Text copyright © 1989 by Virginia Driving Hawk Sneve
Illustrations copyright © 1989 by Stephen Gammell
All rights reserved
Printed in the United States of America

Library of Congress Cataloging-in-Publication Data

Dancing teepees: poems of American Indian youth/selected by Virginia
Driving Hawk Sneve; illustrated by Stephen Gammell.—1st ed.:
p. cm.
Summary: An illustrated collection of poems from the oral tradition
of Native Americans.
ISBN 0-8234-0724-1
1. Children's poetry, Indian—United States—Translations into English. 2.
Indian poetry—Translations into English. 3. American poetry—Translations
from Indian languages. 4. Indians of North America—Juvenile poetry. 5.
Children's poetry, American—Translations from Indian languages. [1.
Indians of North America—Poetry. 2. Indian poetry—Collections.] I. Sneve,
Virginia Driving Hawk. II. Gammell, Stephen, ill.
PM197.E3D36   1989
897—dc19   88-11075   CIP   AC

ISBN 0-8234-0724-1
ISBN 0-8234-0879-5 (pbk.)

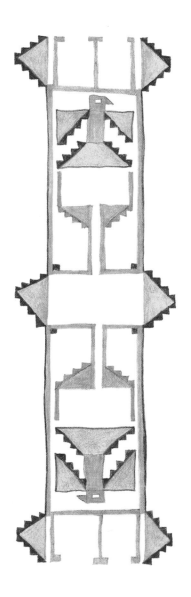

The Indian needs no writings; words that are true sink deep into his heart where they remain; he never forgets them.

Four Guns, Lakota tribal judge

To American Indians, the spoken word was sacred. Children listened to their grandparents tell stories, recite ceremonial prayers and chants, and sing lullabies and other tribal songs. The children grew up remembering this music and knew that the act of speaking words gave life to Native American stories, songs, and prayers. Words were chosen carefully and rarely wasted.

Many of the selections here have been passed from the old to the young. Others are from contemporary tribal poets (including the anthologist), who, as children, learned to respect the power of the spoken word.

Virginia Driving Hawk Sneve

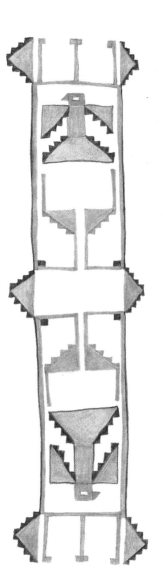

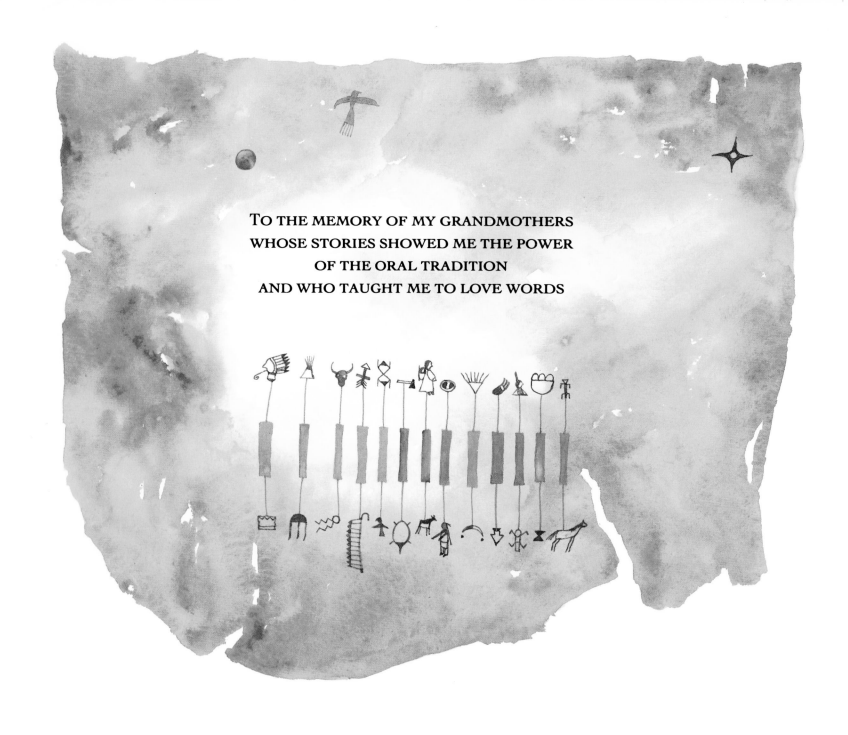

TO THE MEMORY OF MY GRANDMOTHERS
WHOSE STORIES SHOWED ME THE POWER
OF THE ORAL TRADITION
AND WHO TAUGHT ME TO LOVE WORDS

Contents

The Life of a Man Is a Circle	8	The Black Turkey-Gobbler	22
Sun, Moon, Stars	10	My Dress Is Old	23
Tble	11	Farewell, My Younger Brother	24
Puva, Puva, Puva	13	Mother, We Are Cold	25
Coo . . . Ah . . . Coo!	14	The Four Corners of the Universe	26
Nicely, Nicely	15	Far to the West	27
My Little Son	17	I Rise, I Rise	29
I Watched an Eagle Soar	18	My Horse, Fly Like a Bird	30
We Chased Butterflies	19	The Stars Streaming in the Sky	31
Dancing Teepees	20	*Acknowledgments*	32

 The Life of a Man Is a Circle

The life of a man is a circle from childhood
to childhood, and so it is in everything where
power moves. Our teepees were round like the
nests of the birds, and these were always set
in a circle, the nation's hoop, a nest of many nests,
where the Great Spirit meant for us to hatch
our children.

BLACK ELK, LAKOTA SIOUX

 Sun, Moon, Stars

Sun, moon, stars,
You that move in the heavens,
Hear this mother!
A new life has come among you.
Make its life smooth.

FROM AN OMAHA CEREMONY
FOR THE NEWBORN

10

Tble

Tble,
named for the cold star
appearing after the blizzard
ceased its wail.
Hers filled the tent
at life's first shock.
Birth wet, Tble,
Steaming in the frigid air.

VIRGINIA DRIVING HAWK SNEVE

 Puva, Puva, Puva

Puva, puva, puva,
In the trail the beetles
On each other's backs are sleeping,
So on mine, my baby, thou.
Puva, puva, puva!

HOPI LULLABYE

 Coo . . . Ah . . . Coo!

Coo . . . ah . . . Coo!
Little Dove,
The wind is rocking
Thy nest in the pine bough,
My arms are rocking
Thy nest, little Dove.
Coo . . . ah . . . coo!

PAIUTE CRADLE SONG

 Nicely, Nicely

Nicely, nicely, nicely, away in the east,
the rain clouds care for the little corn
    plants
as a mother cares for her baby.

ZUNI CORN CEREMONY

My Little Son

My little son,
you will put a whale harpoon
and a sealing spear into your canoe,
not knowing what use you will make of them.

MAKAH

17

 I Watched an Eagle Soar

Grandmother,
I watched an eagle soar
high in the sky
until a cloud covered him up.
Grandmother,
I still saw the eagle
behind my eyes.

VIRGINIA DRIVING HAWK SNEVE

⋈ We Chased Butterflies

We chased butterflies to give us endurance
in running. After we caught one, we rubbed our hearts
with its wings, saying,
"O, Butterfly, lend me your grace and swiftness!"
That was a boy's first lesson.

PLENTY-COUPS, CROW

▲ Dancing Teepees

Dancing teepees
High up in the Rocky Mountains
Dancing teepees
Dance on the grassy banks of Cripple Creek
With laughing fringes in the autumn sun.
Indian children
Play with bows and arrows
On the grassy banks of Cripple Creek.
Indian women
Gather kindling
To start an evening fire.

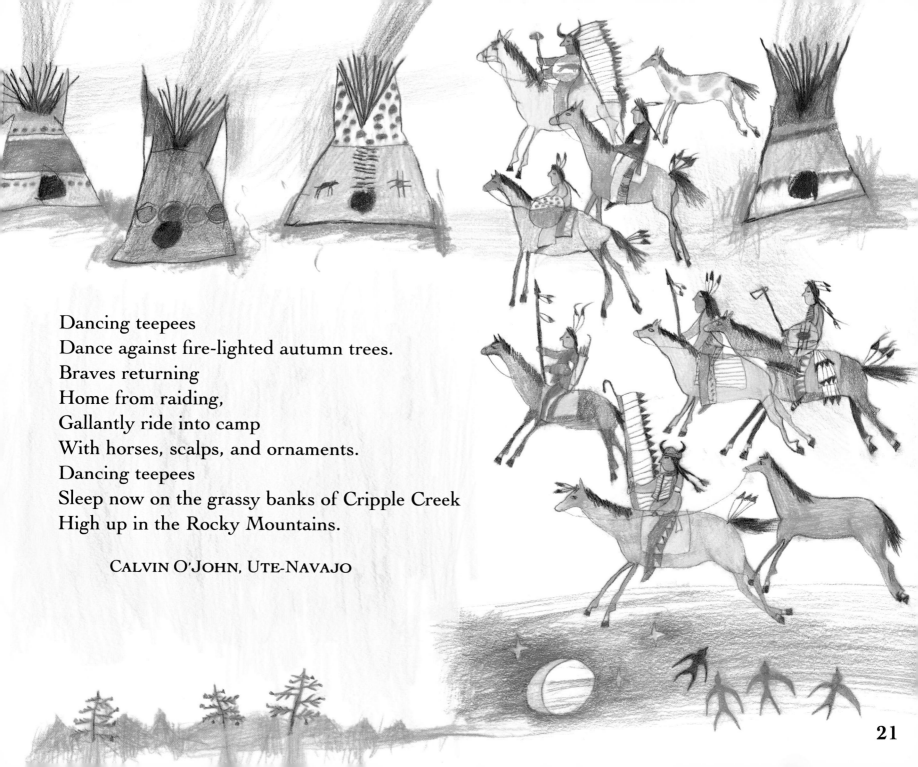

Dancing teepees
Dance against fire-lighted autumn trees.
Braves returning
Home from raiding,
Gallantly ride into camp
With horses, scalps, and ornaments.
Dancing teepees
Sleep now on the grassy banks of Cripple Creek
High up in the Rocky Mountains.

CALVIN O'JOHN, UTE-NAVAJO

21

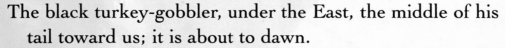

The Black Turkey-Gobbler

The black turkey-gobbler, under the East, the middle of his
   tail toward us; it is about to dawn.
The black turkey-gobbler, the tips of his beautiful tail;
   above us the dawn whitens.
The black turkey-gobbler, the tips of his beautiful tail;
   above us the dawn becomes yellow.
The sunbeams stream forward, dawn boys, with shimmering shoes
   of yellow;
On top of the sunbeams that stream toward us they are
   dancing.
At the East the rainbow moves forward, dawn maidens, with
   shimmering shoes and shirts of yellow dance over us.
Beautifully over us it is dawning.

MESCALERO APACHE

◈ My Dress Is Old

My dress is old, but at night the moon is
   kind.
Then I wear a beautiful moon-colored dress.

TRIBE UNKNOWN

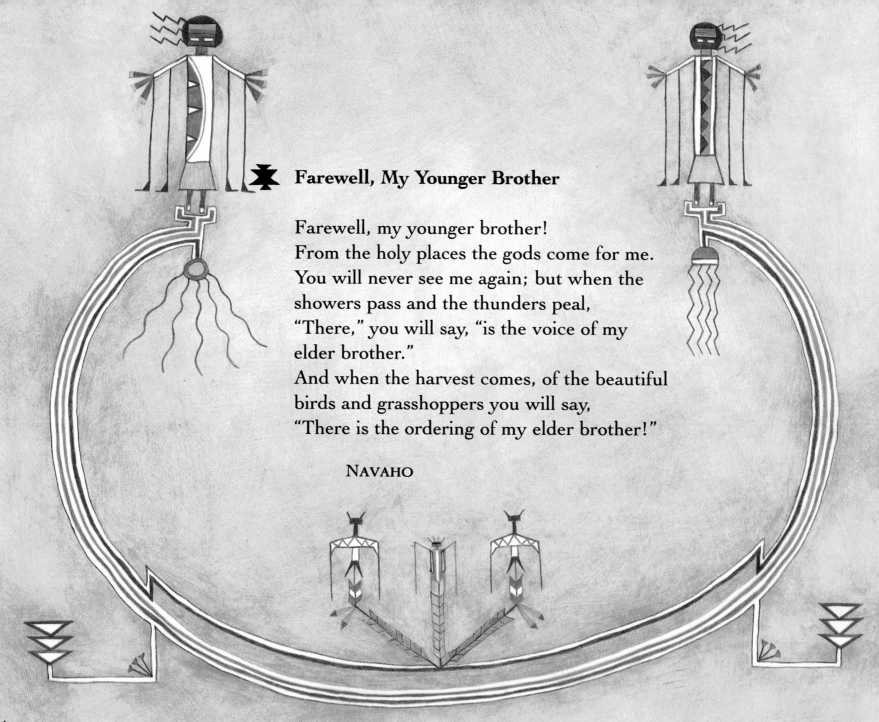

Farewell, My Younger Brother

Farewell, my younger brother!
From the holy places the gods come for me.
You will never see me again; but when the
showers pass and the thunders peal,
"There," you will say, "is the voice of my
elder brother."
And when the harvest comes, of the beautiful
birds and grasshoppers you will say,
"There is the ordering of my elder brother!"

NAVAHO

}◆{ Mother, We Are Cold

Mother, we are cold.
Shall we die upon your breast?
Grandfather, cried Mother,
Must your grandchildren perish
'Neath the winter's snow?
Grandfather clad the trees
In bronze, red, and yellow
For a final dance of swirling leaves
Falling to blanket
The flower nation until spring.

an adaptation of a children's legend,
"WHY THE TREES LOSE THEIR LEAVES,"
by VIRGINIA DRIVING HAWK SNEVE

The Four Corners of the Universe

You will be running to the four corners of
the universe;
To where the land meets the big water;
To where the sky meets the land;
To where the home of winter is;
To the home of rain.
Run!
Be strong.
For you are the mother of a people.

A Song for Young Girls,
Mescalero Apache

Far to the West

Far to the west,
Far by the sky
Stands a blue elk.
That elk standing yonder
Watches over all the daughters
On the earth.

DAKOTA ELK SONG

🐃 I Rise, I Rise

I rise, I rise,
I, whose tread makes the earth to rumble.
I rise, I rise,
I, in whose thighs there is strength.
I rise, I rise,
I, who whips his back with his tail when in
  rage.
I rise, I rise,
I, in whose humped shoulder there is
  power.
I rise, I rise,
I, who shakes his mane when angered.
I rise, I rise,
I, whose horns are sharp and curved.

FROM AN OSAGE PRAYER BEFORE
A YOUNG MAN'S FIRST BUFFALO HUNT

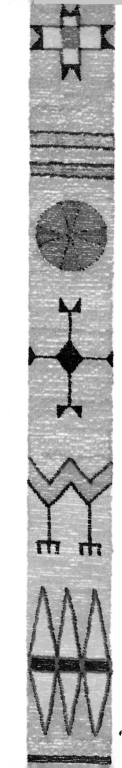

My Horse, Fly Like a Bird

My horse, fly like a bird
To carry me far
From the arrows of my enemies,
And I will tie red ribbons
To your streaming hair.

VIRGINIA DRIVING HAWK SNEVE
adapted from a Lakota warrior's
song to his horse

The Stars Streaming in the Sky

The stars streaming in the sky are my hair.
The round rim of the earth which you see
Binds my starry hair.

FROM THE CREATION MYTH
OF THE WINTU

Acknowledgments

Grateful acknowledgment is made for the following reprints: "The Black Turkey Gobbler" titled "Black Turkey in the East" from *Gotal —A Mescalero Apache Ceremony* by Pliny E. Goddard. *Putnam Anniversary Vol.*, G.E. Stechert & Co., N.Y., 1909.

"Coo...Ah...Coo!" titled "Paiute Cradle Song" from *The American Rhythm*. Permission granted by Cooper Square Publishers, Totowa, New Jersey.

"Dancing Teepees" by Calvin O'John from *The Whispering Wind* edited by Terry Allen. Copyright © 1972 by The Institute of American Indian Arts. Reprinted by permission of Doubleday, a division of Bantam, Doubleday, Dell Publishing Group, Inc.

"Far to the West" titled "Elk Song" from *The Indians' Book*, Natalie Curtis, Dover Publications, Inc., 1968.

"Farewell, My Younger Brother" by permission of Smithsonian Institution Press from *Fifth Annual Report of the Bureau of American Ethnology 1883–1884*. Smithsonian Institution, Washington, D.C.

"The Four Corners of the Universe" from "Singing for Life, The Mescalero Apache Puberty Ceremony," Southwestern Indian Ritual Drama, University of New Mexico Press, 1980. Used by permission of Claire R. Farrer, author.

"I Rise, I Rise" by permission of Smithsonian Institution Press from *Thirty-ninth Annual Report of the Bureau of American Ethnology 1917–18*. Smithsonian Institution, Washington, D.C. 1925.

"The Indian Needs No Writings" from *Red Man Reservations* by Clark Wissler. Reprinted by permission of Macmillan Publishing Company.

"The Life of a Man Is a Circle" from *Black Elk Speaks* by John G. Neihardt, copyright John G. Neihardt 1932, 1959, 1961, published by Simon & Schuster Pocket Books and the University of Nebraska Press.

"My Dress Is Old" from "Little Indians Speak" from *The Gift Is Rich* by E. Russell Carter, Friendship Press, New York. Copyright © 1951. Used by permission.

"My Little Son" by permission of Smithsonian Institution Press from *Bureau of American Ethnology Bulletin 24*. Smithsonian Institution, Washington, D.C. 1894.

"Nicely, Nicely" by permission of Smithsonian Institution Press from *Fifth Annual Report of the Bureau of American Ethnology 1883–84*. Smithsonian Institution, Washington, D.C. 1887.

"Puva, Puva, Puva" titled "Hopi Lullaby" from *The Indians' Book*, Natalie Curtis. Dover Publications, Inc., 1968.

"The Stars Streaming in the Sky" from "Wintu: The North Star" by William Brandon from *The Magic World*. Reprinted by permission of Harold Ober Associates Incorporated. Copyright © 1971 by William Brandon.

"Sun, Moon, Stars" by permission of Smithsonian Institution Press from *Twenty-seventh Annual Report of the Bureau of American Ethnology 1905–06*. Smithsonian Institution, Washington, D.C. 1911.

"We Chased Butterflies" originally titled "Butterfly Chasing" from *Plenty-Coups, Chief of the Crows* by Frank Bird Linderman. Reprinted by permission of Harper & Row, Publishers.